our generation®

This is Lily Anna's story.

LILY ANNA™

ADVENTURES AT SHELBY STABLES

BY

JULIE DRISCOLL

ILLUSTRATED BY KRISTI VALIANT

An Our Generation® *book*

BATTAT INCORPORATED *Publisher*

A very special thanks to the editor,
Joanne Burke Casey.

For Madeline and Ted

CONTENTS

EXTRA! EXTRA! READ ALL ABOUT IT!
Big words, wacky words, powerful words, funny words...
*what do they all mean? They are marked with this symbol * .*
Look them up in the Glossary at the end of this book.

Chapter One

SHY, SUPERSTITIOUS SLEEPWALKER

I fumbled in the darkness feeling for the light switch on the wall. Click! My eyes squinted to adjust to the sudden brightness. Delia, my stuffed horse, peered out from under my pillow as if to say, "What do you think you're doing?"

My little sister Ida rolled over and scrunched her face into her pillow. She's a sound sleeper. But wait! *Where's my bed?* I wondered. *What happened to it and why are Ida and I sleeping on mattresses on the floor?*

I slid my feet into my fuzzy horse slippers. They matched my pink horse pajamas. Then I made my way down the hallway. I came to my brother Sam's room. It was dark so I reached in and switched on the light. I stumbled over some boxes in the hallway. *Maybe my bed is in here,* I thought.

"*Mooom,*" groaned Sam, "she's doing it again."

I rummaged* through the boxes, searching for my bed. My mom appeared in front of me and shook me gently. I ignored her, though.

"Lily Anna! Wake up. You're sleepwalking."

I stared at her blankly, and then—like pushing a button on a radio to get a signal—everything became clear to me.

"Go back to bed," whispered my mom.

I shrugged my shoulders and, without uttering a word, returned to my room and settled back onto my mattress on the floor.

My mom followed me and turned off the light. "Get some sleep. The movers are arriving bright and early."

I lay on my mattress with my eyes closed, but all of a sudden I was wide awake. *Darn!* I thought. *If they would only not wake me up from my sleepwalking then I wouldn't have trouble falling back to sleep.*

I picked up Delia and squeezed her tight. She's a small gray stuffed horse with a white mane and tail and round, shiny black eyes. When I hug her *really* tight she squeaks. My Grandpa Ted and Grandma Madeline gave her to me, along with all the other horse stuff that I own. They're obsessed* with horses. Which suddenly reminded me…

I reached over and felt around for my horseshoe necklace. I'd left it leaning against the wall, with the horseshoe facing upward for good luck. Yep. It was still facing up, as it should be. Grandma told me that a horseshoe facing upward helps keep all the luck in. And I needed all the luck I could get.

Tomorrow we would be moving from our big

old brownstone* in the city to my grandparents' horse ranch in the country—Shelby Stables, to be exact. Grandpa and Grandma were getting on in years and the ranch was becoming too much for them to manage on their own.

Mom missed the ranch and Dad agreed that a change from the city life would be good. So there I was, lying on a mattress on the floor, thinking that my life was about to change *drastically**.

I thought about the life that I was leaving behind. *Will anyone at Greenview Elementary even notice I'm gone on Monday?* I wondered. I'm so quiet, I'll bet no one will—no one except for my friends Mari and Rose.

Mari and Rose are the only two girls at my school who didn't seem to mind my shyness. Perhaps it was because they were a little quiet themselves and therefore, understood me.

Sometimes, at lunch, I'd hardly say a word—not because I didn't have anything to say. Oh no! I have lots of stuff going on in my head—lots and lots. But something happens from the point where I have a thought to where it should then come out of my mouth. It never does.

And on occasion, when I do speak, I feel very awkward. I feel like running away, like one of the wild horses on my pajamas—running and running, never looking back.

I hoped I'd meet some girls at the new school who would be nice and understand me the way that Mari and Rose did. Two quiet girls just like me. I stretched my arm out from under the covers and knocked on the wood floor three times.

So, I guess there are a few things you should know about me right up front in case you haven't already figured them out. I'm superstitious*. I don't know why, but I just am. And I'm shy—very shy.

My brother Sam calls me the shy, superstitious sleepwalker. And Ida even made up a song about me.

*"Shy, superstitious girl—walks in her sleep
Shy, superstitious girl—who doesn't speak."*

Ida can't help herself. She makes up songs about

everyone. Even our paperboy has a song.

I was sad about leaving the city and everything there that was comfortable and familiar to me. But part of me was excited, too. Aside from the long car ride, I always enjoyed visiting Grandma and Grandpa.

I could still smell the ranch in my head: hay, horse manure, moldy wood and leather, with lilacs in the spring and roses in the summertime. And I have so many good memories such as picking apples from their orchard, sledding on the big hill beside the barn and swimming in the pond near my great uncle Moe's farm.

Moe is Grandpa Ted's brother. They don't really speak to one another and I'm not sure why.

I couldn't wait to go back to the ranch. But I wondered how it would be to actually live there. *Yaaawn.* A shy, superstitious sleepwalker moving to the country to live on a farm—*tomorrow*. I couldn't believe it was tomorrow!

I noticed light peeking through the window shades. I yawned again. My eyelids felt heavy. A very sleepy, shy, superstitious sleepwalker *finally*…asleep.

Chapter Two

HOME SWEET RANCH

I don't remember much of the car ride to the ranch because I slept almost the entire way. I awoke to Ida, her usual perky* self, singing an annoying song. Sam was begging her to stop.

> *"Oh I've got a song that gets on everybody's nerves, everybody's nerves, everybody's nerves. Oh I've got a song that gets on everybody's nerves and this is how it goes..."*

Over and over again...

When she noticed I was awake she perked up even more. "Look Lily Anna!" She pointed to the big round fly that was bouncing about on the back of the car window. "That fly came with us all the way from the city. I named him Bob."

I smiled. Still groggy* and tired, I rubbed my eyes and stared out the car window. *We're definitely in cow country,* I thought, as we passed a large stretch of green pasture* filled with black-and-white cows. Many of them were lying down.

"It's going to rain," I said.

Dad peered over the steering wheel and gazed up at the fluffy white clouds. "It doesn't look like rain to me."

"You and your superstitions," said Sam, knowing why I'd said it.

I ignored them. I knew that cows lying down was a sign it was going to rain.

Before long we were turning onto the dusty road that led to Shelby Stables. We passed Moe's farm at the beginning of the road on the left. Shelby Stables and Moe's farm used to be one big plot* of land owned by my great grandfather.

After my great grandfather passed away*, Grandpa and Moe split the land. Grandpa got the land way up at the top of the hill with the apple orchard on it. He built a big ranch house and an even bigger red barn on

the property.

When we sit on the front porch of the ranch house, way up on that hill, we can see for miles.

Moe kept the land with the old house and barn that he and Grandpa grew up in. I think it's strange that they don't speak. In all the years I've visited the ranch, I've never once met Moe.

Our car bounced and jerked over the gravel and dirt as we drove up the hill. A white fence lined both sides of the road. On the right was one of three paddocks* that Grandpa built so the horses could run about and graze*.

I saw my favorite apple tree at the other side of the paddock, next to the barn. I call it the lone apple tree because it's all by itself, far away from the apple orchard that covers the hilly backside of the ranch.

There was one horse grazing inside the paddock. He was a beautiful bay* horse with a white blaze* running down his face. Our car startled him and he jumped up and did a little sidestep.

When we last visited the ranch, about a year ago, Grandpa tried to teach Ida and me to ride. Sam has already been riding for a few years now. Grandpa chose his gentlest horse for me but I was still scared. Sitting way up high on that large creature intimidated* me a little and I got the sense the horse knew I was scared.

I didn't even make it a few feet from the barn when I cried to Grandpa to take me off the horse. Ida did OK though, and went for a short walk around the stables with Grandpa.

I loved horses. I loved patting them, feeding them, brushing them and even just watching them. Riding them was a different story.

I finally decided it would be a little strange for me to live on a horse ranch and not know how to ride. So a few weeks ago, when I spoke to Grandma and Grandpa on the phone, I told them that I was ready to take lessons.

They scheduled my first lesson with Cookie, one of the trainers, for the day after our arrival. I was beginning to wonder if I shouldn't have spoken so quickly.

From the dirt road I could see Charlie, Grandpa's ranch hand*, entering the side door of the barn. His dog Bagel spotted our car, charged full speed toward us, and chased us the rest of the way up the hill.

Charlie had originally named his dog Regal, the beagle, but because of his heavy accent it always sounded like he was saying Ragle, the bagel. So the name Bagel sort of stuck.

Straight up the hill, to the left of the big red barn, was the ranch house. The moving truck was already there and we pulled up alongside it. The movers were lifting my bed off the truck.

When I stepped out of the car, my body felt all twisted and sore from sitting for so long. Grandma and Grandpa greeted us with hugs and kisses.

Grandma was a petite woman with white hair that she wore pulled back in a tight ponytail. She always smelled like a loaf of freshly baked bread and clothes that had been hanging on a clothesline for days.

Grandpa was very rugged* looking with lots of lines on his face and a year-round tan.

Ida left the car door open for Bob, the fly. He finally

buzzed his way out the passenger door and took off toward Moe's. "Enjoy your new home," Ida said in her usual half-singing, half-speaking voice.

Charlie yelled over from the barn and waved hello. I waved back. The sky beyond where he was standing had turned a deep, purplish gray. I knew it was going to rain.

Grandpa seemed to know, too, and yelled to Charlie to bring the horse in from the paddock. Shortly after, a great flash of lightning lit up the sky and drops of rain began hitting the ground like pellets*. The horse paced nervously.

"Never in all my years have I met a horse as spooked by everything as this one is," said Grandpa as he shook his head and headed toward the barn.

Grandma put her arms around Ida and me, squeezed us into her sides and walked us up onto the front porch. A familiar sign that read "Home Sweet Ranch" hung over the front door and the movers walked briskly* by, carrying pieces of my bed. I knew where they were headed—last room, down the hall on the right—the one with the best view of the apple orchard.

The ranch house was large enough that I wasn't going to have to share a room with Ida anymore. Grandma and Grandpa had cleared all the old furniture out of our bedrooms. They painted my room a soft pink. Ida's room was also painted. She had asked them to paint it the brightest yellow they could find.

"Do you know it's good luck to move into a new home during a rainstorm?" asked Grandma.

I nodded. I actually did know that.

Ida and I stood on the porch and watched as Grandpa and Charlie tried to lead the horse into the barn. The horse was jerking his head up and down and tugging on his lead line*.

Another streak of lightning zigzagged through the sky. It was quickly followed by a loud boom of thunder. The horse broke away from Charlie's grasp and took off in a gallop* around the paddock.

Sam ran down and held open the door that led from the paddock to the barn. Dad went to help, too.

The horse galloped by but was too spooked to enter. It didn't help that Bagel was near the barn door barking at Grandpa, Charlie and the horse. Grandpa and Charlie tried to approach the horse but he reared up* on his hind legs and let out a big whinny*.

It had begun raining even harder and the horse seemed even *more* frightened.

Chapter Three

THE SOUR HORSE

By the time they finally got the horse inside the barn, Charlie, Grandpa and my dad were soaking wet and covered up to their knees in mud. I felt sorry for the horse. He had put up such a fight.

Ida and I ran down to the barn and stood at the side entrance to watch as they led the horse into his stall and closed the door behind him. The horse was still disturbed and continued to neigh* and circle round and round. This seemed to make all the other horses in the barn nervous.

"What's his name?" I asked Charlie, as I hoisted* myself up on the wooden slats of his stall door and leaned over the top rail.

"Cooper Cream," he replied. "But don't get too attached. We're not keeping him."

"Why not?" I asked.

"That horse can't be trained!" exclaimed Charlie. "He's been here two weeks and we don't know what to do with him. He doesn't want to be around other horses, which is why he has that paddock all to himself and we can't saddle him up.

"He's bad-tempered—what we call a sour horse," said Charlie as he hung a halter* on a nearby hook and walked slowly and tiredly out of the barn, "a sour horse indeed."

"Cooper Cream, that has a nice ring to it," I said, as I gazed at the sour horse. Ida agreed and broke out in a song.

"Cooper Cream, you're a dream
Cooper Cream, please don't scream!"

Ida's singing seemed to settle Cooper Cream's nerves. He stopped circling and stood at the far end of his stall, staring at me.

"Keep singing," I told her. "He likes it."

Ida began singing and dancing up and down the wide corridor of the barn. Many of the horses poked their heads out of their stalls to see what all

the commotion* was about.

Cooper Cream remained at the back of his stall. His big brown eyes blinked and his head hung low. I got some hay and held it out to him but he didn't budge.

In many ways he reminded me of *me*. I was new just like him. And I was easily spooked, too, particularly when it came to riding.

Tomorrow would be my first day of school. I felt a little like Cooper Cream—like a horse that was about to be broken in*.

Chapter Four

KNOCK ON WOOD

After school I hurried to the barn. It was a spacious* barn with a tack* room for storing the saddles and bridles on one end and a long row of stalls at the other end. Some of the stalls were rented out to owners who needed a place to board* their horses.

A few of Grandma and Grandpa's horses like Goldie, Prince and Nutmeg had been living at the ranch for as long as I could remember. I was going to be taking lessons on Goldie later that day.

Cooper Cream's stall was the last one on the right. Charlie was leading him out to the paddock. I followed them and collapsed under the lone apple tree. I let out a big sigh of relief, glad that the school day was behind me.

It had been an awful first day. I'd packed my

lucky pencil and pen, wore my lucky horseshoe necklace and even ate my lucky breakfast—a glass of apple juice and five mini pizza bagels. Five is my lucky number and I'll eat pizza anytime of day. But nothing I did seemed to matter.

The library was probably the worst part of my day. There were two girls sitting quietly at a table. They reminded me of Mari and Rose. I sat down beside them but they were too busy giggling and scribbling things in a notebook to notice me.

At one point, one of the girls glanced quickly up at me and then, just as quickly, went back to her friend and their giggling and scribbling.

Lunch was no picnic either. I couldn't stand the thought of sitting all by myself so I made up an excuse to go to my locker.

While I was at my locker a girl approached. She opened her locker door a few spaces from mine. I remembered her from the bus ride to school earlier that morning. She was hard to miss.

When she had boarded the bus I was distracted by a jingling noise and the bright green scally cap* she wore on her head. Her thick wavy hair was pulled back in a ponytail and tucked up under it.

Her backpack was the usual design with zippers and pockets. But hanging off one of the side buckles were a gazillion key chains. They clanked against the corners of the seat cushions as she forged* her way to an empty seat behind Ida and me.

I stood at my locker pretending not to notice her and pretending I was getting something from inside it.

She opened her locker door. It was overflowing with books, papers and junk. Using all her strength she pulled her backpack from her locker and plunked it down on the floor.

"Here they are!" she said, whipping out a stack of bright red paper. Then she shoved the backpack back inside the locker.

As she used her entire body to force the door to close behind her she turned toward me. "Here, have one," she said, handing me a red piece of paper. "I'm hanging these around the school. Are you new?"

"Yes, I…."

R-R-R-I-I-N-N-N-G

The school bell sounded, signaling that it was time for the next class.

"Gotta go. I only have a few minutes to hang these." She smiled and hurried down the long hallway that was quickly filling up with kids.

I didn't mind that we were interrupted by the bell. I knew she wasn't the type of girl who'd want to be friends with me anyhow.

I glanced down at the flier. It read:

Cranberry Hill JAMBOREE* CONCERT
Saturday Night at the Sugarberry Stage
Potluck*
Tie your horses in the rear!

I tucked it away inside my notebook and headed to my next class.

⚜ ⚜

I sat on the grass trying to erase the day from my memory. Pretty little apple blossoms had fallen to the ground, surrounding the tree like a blanket.

Cooper Cream was grazing on a patch of grass

nearby. I began humming the words to the song that Ida had made up.

Cooper Cream raised his head and walked slowly toward me. I stopped singing and stared up at him. He nodded his head up and down and then stomped his right hoof. It was as though he was telling me to continue singing. So I did.

When I stopped singing he began nodding and pawing again. This made me laugh. I held out a slice of apple that I'd brought with me from the house.

He moved closer and spread his nostrils to sniff it. Then he snatched it from my hand with his mouth and began chomping* on it.

For the next hour I forgot all about the terrible day I'd had. Cooper Cream and I played our little singing game. He seemed to enjoy it, too. It was as if we'd established our own way of speaking to one another.

I stood on the rail of the fence and patted his long, soft neck. He was so big yet seemed so gentle. I couldn't tell by his eyes whether he was happy or sad but I sensed that he somehow trusted me and wanted to be my friend.

The blue pickup truck that was rattling up the hill startled Cooper Cream. He jerked his head and neighed.

"Shhhh," I reassured him. "It's only Cookie."

Cooper Cream seemed to understand what I'd said and settled down.

Cookie was going to teach me to ride. She's been working at Shelby Stables for a few years now. She also boards her own horse, Ginger, at the ranch.

Everyone calls her Cookie because her last name is Cook. I don't even know her first name. I've only known her as Cookie.

I said goodbye to Cooper Cream and ran to the barn to get my helmet, riding gloves and boots.

I was feeling a little anxious about my riding lesson. Goldie, the horse I was going to be training on, was a dappled* gray horse with a dark mane and tail. She seemed gentle enough but I still couldn't get rid of the knots in my stomach.

Cookie stopped to speak with Grandpa outside the barn. While I waited, I paced nervously back and forth.

She's a good horse, I told myself. *I'm going to be a great rider!*

I decided I should knock on wood—just to make it real—so I knocked on the wooden beam of Goldie's stall three times. Then, for the fun of it, I began walking from stall to stall, knocking three times on the beams, singing the words to Cooper Cream's song as I went along. When I reached the last stall, I suddenly had a strange feeling that someone was watching me. I turned quickly.

Standing at the far end of the barn was the girl from school—the one with the gazillion key chains.

Chapter Five

CART BEFORE THE HORSE

I stood frozen in position, staring at the girl. I could feel that my face was beet red as she walked toward me.

"You're a good singer," she said matter-of-factly. She stopped at one of the nearby stalls and patted the horse inside it.

I was speechless.

"I'm Rachel and this is my horse, Scout. I saw you at school today."

I nodded.

"Are you boarding your horse here?" she asked.

"No," I replied. "This is my grandpa's ranch. We're going to be living here now."

She seemed surprised. "So you're Mr. Shelby's granddaughter? What's your name?"

"Lily Anna," I muttered*. "And this is Goldie.

I'm starting lessons with her today."

Cookie entered the barn and interrupted us. She was all business, as though she'd seen me just yesterday and not for the first time in over a year. "Hey ya. You ready for your lesson?"

I nodded.

"OK then, let's get Goldie readied."

I smiled at Rachel and followed Cookie to the tack room.

The next hour of my lesson wasn't too bad. Cookie taught me how to tack up* the horse. First we brushed Goldie's coat and cleaned out her hoofs.

Then we placed a saddle pad* on the horse's back, followed by the saddle*. We wrapped the girth* around the horse's belly and tightened it.

We fastened the bridle* in place and led Goldie to the outdoor ring. Cookie showed me how to lunge* the horse by holding the lunge line* and letting the horse circle around me. This all seemed fairly easy.

But when it came time for me to sit up on the horse, I froze.

"Just place your left foot in the stirrup*," Cookie explained, "then quickly pull yourself up and swing your right leg over."

Goldie stood patiently while I fumbled to get up on her. I was way up high on the horse and I held onto the reins* as though my life depended upon it. I was squeezing Goldie so hard with my legs I thought I might hurt her.

Rachel was leading Scout into the barn and saw how scared I was. Cookie noticed, too, and didn't make me stay up there for very long.

"OK missy, that's enough for today," she said, helping me off the horse. My legs felt all wobbly but I was happy when my feet finally touched the ground again.

Afterward, while I was in the tack room, Rachel entered.

"So, I noticed you're afraid of horses!"

"Yeah," I admitted. "But only when it comes to

riding them. I like them just fine other than that."

"Hmmm," she said placing her fingers on her chin. "I think what you need is the apple cart lesson."

Huh, I thought. I didn't actually say "Huh" but my expression must have said it for me.

"Come on," she commanded. "I'll show you."

I followed her outside, to the back of the barn. The apple trees, with their pretty, pinkish-white blossoms were lined up in perfect rows covering the entire backside of the farm.

She grabbed the apple cart that was parked beside the barn and wheeled it toward me. "Get in!" she commanded.

I obeyed and climbed inside the cart.

The next thing I knew, we were flying down the hill weaving in and out of the trees. I was giggling as I gripped the sides of the cart. Rachel was laughing, too, as she pushed me down the hill.

When we got to the bottom of the hill, Rachel slowed the cart to a halt and paused to catch her breath. "OK now, get out and help me push this thing back up the hill."

I took one of the wooden handles. Rachel held the other and together we pushed the apple cart back up the hill toward the barn.

"Now," she said when we reached the top, "I'm going to get in and *you're* going to push *me*."

"OK," I agreed.

Rachel sat confidently in the cart as I wheeled her down the hill. I steered the cart between and around the trees. As we neared the bottom, the cart began to pick up speed.

It became more difficult for me to control the cart and I was afraid it was going to get away from me. I made a quick decision and tipped the cart to its side to bring it to a stop. Rachel spilled out onto the grass. We both lay on the ground laughing.

"So, did you get the lesson I just taught you?" she asked.

Still catching my breath, I shook my head.

"OK, here's the lesson," she said. "First, I pushed you in the cart. That symbolized* that you were *indeed* learning something—like how to push a cart or ride a horse, for example—and I was the one teaching you.

"Next, we pushed the cart together, meaning that you were *indeed* ready to take the next step and push the cart with my help. Finally, it was your turn to push the cart all by yourself. And you did, except I was in the cart this time. Do you know why?"

"No," I replied.

"Because even though you were *indeed* ready to push the cart on your own, I was still there, right inside the cart, just in case you needed me. The same goes for riding a horse. You'll see!"

"Why do you keep saying *indeed*?" I asked her.

"That's one of my new words. I'm trying it out."

"Oh," I said. I paused for a moment and thought about how different she was from Mari and Rose. She had a pretty face with freckles that matched her long brown hair, which had come untucked from her scally cap.

"Why do you have so many key chains on your backpack?" I asked her.

"My father travels a lot. Whenever he's in a new city or country, he buys me a key chain. It's our little thing."

I smiled. "I like the apple cart scenario*," I told her.

"I liked it too, up until the point where you tossed me out onto the grass!"

We laughed and I knew right then that Rachel and I would *indeed* become good friends.

Chapter Six

RAINY SEASON

A lot had happened in the two weeks since we first moved to Shelby Stables. I'd finally overcome my fear of riding and was now able to take Goldie for a slow trot around the ring.

Cookie was pleased and told me that, in a few weeks, I'd be ready to start learning jumps. Riding a horse was becoming second nature to me.

And Rachel and I did, *indeed*, become good friends. She didn't mind that I didn't talk a lot. She did enough talking for the two of us. Rachel was at the stable nearly every day.

On the days that I didn't have my lessons, Rachel and Scout would ride with Goldie and me around the ring.

"Just like the apple cart lesson," she'd say. "Soon

you'll be doing this all by yourself." And she was right!

So I could help pay for my riding lessons, Charlie taught me how to clean the horses' stalls and care for them. Each day I brought the horses fresh hay and water, brushed their coats and manes, picked out dirt and rocks from their hoofs. I even sang to them.

Cooper Cream loved it when I sang to him while I brushed his reddish-brown coat. I always spent extra time with him.

Each day, when I entered the barn to do my chores, Cooper Cream would begin neighing as soon as he heard my voice, as if to say "come and see me first." I always did. I'd grown very attached to that horse.

When we weren't tending to the horses and cleaning the stalls, Rachel, Ida and I would sneak up to our fort in the loft* above the barn. We called it Lemon Loft.

Ida would mix up a large jug of lemonade and haul it up to the loft while Rachel and I finished our chores. It was our very own lemonade stand in the sky.

We'd open the doors to the loft that overlooked the dirt driveway. Then we'd yell down to anyone entering and exiting the barn, "Sir, Ma'am, would you like some lemonade? It's 25 cents, or free if you say the magic word!"

Charlie always played along. He'd reply, "Why, yes *indeed* I would like some lemonade!"

Indeed was the magic word that you needed to say to get the lemonade and Charlie knew it.

We attached a bucket to a long rope and lowered it down to Charlie. He'd reach in and remove his cup of lemonade from the bucket. Sometimes he'd place something in the bucket to send back up to us like one of his special buttons.

Charlie had an entire collection of buttons with horse sayings on them. Rachel, Ida and I decided to start our own collection and many of the buttons hung on a blue ribbon on the wall of our fort. I attached one to my backpack that said "Horses rule!" Rachel wore one on her scally cap that read "My horse ate my homework."

It was a cloudy day. Rachel, Ida, Sam and I climbed off the bus and headed up the long dirt road toward the ranch.

Drops of rain began hitting my nose and cheeks.

"It's rainy season 'round here," complained Rachel. "Seems like all it does is rain, rain, rain." Her key chains rattled against her body and weighed down her backpack so that she was practically dragging it up the hill behind her.

"I'll bet the flowers like the rainy season," said Ida.

I remembered that Cooper Cream didn't like rain and I hoped that Charlie had thought to bring him inside from the paddock.

We walked briskly up the hill. The small drops had turned into loud pattering.

As we neared the ranch I noticed a horse trailer parked beside the barn. Charlie was leading Cooper Cream from the barn toward Grandpa who was standing beside the trailer.

I suddenly realized what was happening and my heart sank. I sprinted up the hill. "No! You can't! You can't send him away!" I cried.

By the time I reached the trailer I was sobbing so hard I'd made more tears than the rain that was whipping against my face.

And I don't know if it was the rain, the dark trailer or my crying that scared him, but Cooper Cream suddenly panicked. He began struggling and trying to back up.

"Why Grandpa? Why?" I cried.

Grandpa didn't answer me. He was too busy trying to help control Cooper Cream who suddenly reared up on his hind legs and came down so hard I thought he was going to trample Charlie and Grandpa. His eyes were opened wide and they had the look of fright in them. I'd never seen him so scared.

Cooper Cream was tugging at the lead line, trying to break away. He reared again and this time, his front hoof hit Charlie's hand. Charlie was forced to let go of the strap.

Cooper Cream took off like a flash of lightning down the dirt road. I started to chase him but Sam and Rachel held me back.

I was soaked by the rain—we all were. But I was too upset to care.

Minutes passed. I was still sobbing. We all stood on the front porch trying to spot Cooper Cream in the distance.

Ida spotted him first. "He's coming back!" she cried. "Someone's bringing him up the hill!"

A tall dark figure led Cooper Cream slowly up

the road. He wore a long black coat and a rimmed hat. Steam was rising up from the ground around them and they both had a shine to them from being soaked by the rain. Grandpa stepped off the porch to greet them.

Cooper Cream seemed unusually calm as the man approached Grandpa and handed him the lead line.

"Thanks Moe," said Grandpa.

Moe tipped his hat, as if to say "you're welcome." Then he turned to walk away.

"Please Grandpa," I begged. "Please don't send Cooper Cream away!"

"We can't keep him," Grandpa explained. "You need to understand. This is my business." Then he led Cooper Cream into the trailer. Cooper Cream went willingly.

I stood there in the rain, crying, as Charlie jumped into the driver's seat of the truck and started up the engine. The trailer, carrying my friend Cooper Cream, disappeared down the long road, into the fog and rain.

Chapter Seven

PLANTING SEEDS

I cried in my bedroom for over an hour. I couldn't stop thinking about Cooper Cream and how scared he seemed. Rachel tried to cheer me up but finally decided I needed time alone.

A while later, my mom knocked on my bedroom door.

"Come with me," she said. "I need your help with something."

I followed her outside to the lone apple tree near the paddock.

"Do you know your grandma helped me plant this tree?" she asked.

I nodded.

"I remember that day like it was yesterday," she said. "I was very sad because your grandpa had decided to sell a horse that I'd grown very attached to.

"Living on a horse ranch and watching as horses come and go can be frustrating at times. Sometimes I felt as though this tree was the only thing I could count on. I watered it, cared for it, and now look at it."

The tree, still wet from the rain, sparkled and glittered in the sunlight.

My mom handed me a small shovel. "I want you to plant your own tree right beside it."

We knelt down a few feet from the tree and I dug a hole. Mom held out the tiny seeds and I placed them in the ground.

"What was the horse's name, the one Grandpa didn't keep?" I asked.

"Chloe," said my mom. "It was a long time ago. This barn hadn't even been built yet—just the ranch house."

"Where did they put the horses?" I asked curiously.

"In Moe's barn at the bottom of the hill. It was before they decided to split the land.

"Every day, after school, I'd run down the hill to the barn to visit Chloe. Everyone at the barn thought she was a sour horse, too. But I didn't think so. To me, she was just scared.

"Moe had been trying out new ways to tame horses. He believed that some of the traditional* methods of breaking a horse were cruel.

"But Grandpa wanted to keep things the same— the way your great grandfather had taught them. 'It's been working for us for years,' he'd say. 'Why change it now?'

"And although Moe felt differently, Grandpa was the eldest, and was in charge of making those decisions."

Mom patted the soil over the seeds. "For some reason, Chloe was frightened of paper. She also wasn't crazy about Jasper, Grandpa's ranch hand at the time. Whenever she saw paper, she'd run like the wind in the other direction. And when Jasper entered the barn she'd whinny and pin her ears back. She never let anyone ride her.

"Moe began working with Chloe using some of the new and gentler methods he'd been reading about. Some people refer to it as horse whispering—a way to earn the horse's trust without harming or frightening it. He believed Chloe had just gotten off to a bad start and that she needed to regain her confidence in people.

"I loved watching Moe as he worked with Chloe. And she responded well. Within a few days, she'd become tame enough that Moe was able to saddle her up and ride her around the paddock—

something no one else had been able to do before.

"One afternoon, I begged Moe to let me ride her. I was already a skilled rider so he agreed.

"I was trotting* Chloe slowly around the paddock when Jasper approached. He had some papers in his hand. Chloe, upon seeing Jasper and the papers, got spooked. She reared up and I got thrown from her.

"It wasn't Chloe's fault, or Moe's. She still hadn't overcome her fear of paper and of Jasper.

"Shortly after, Grandpa sold Chloe. He and Moe split the land and that's when Grandpa built this barn. They barely spoke after that.

"The only time they ever speak is when Grandpa gets a new horse at the barn. Somehow, on the day after they arrive, one or two of them always ends up down the hill in Moe's paddock."

"Who puts them there?" I asked.

"Nobody knows," said my mom. "Grandpa accuses Moe of stealing his horses and Moe claims it's Grandpa playing practical jokes on him. They've been arguing about it for years."

"Why doesn't Moe have any horses or animals in his barn?" I asked.

"I'm not sure," said my mom.

We placed the garden tools inside a bucket. Then my mom went up to the house to start dinner.

I stood and stretched my legs. As I gazed out toward Moe's I noticed a beautiful rainbow had formed in the sky just beyond his barn.

Who, I wondered, *was responsible for moving Grandpa's new horses to Moe's barn?*

I quickly decided that solving the mystery of the stolen horses would be a good way for me to take my mind off Cooper Cream.

I raced up to the loft to tell Rachel and Ida all about the stolen horses and the feud* between Grandpa and Moe.

Chapter Eight

THE PLAN

Almost two months had passed and we were still trying to solve the mystery of the missing horses. Rachel and I had spoken with everyone who might know something about it—everyone except Moe. For some reason, we couldn't get up the nerve to talk to him about it.

Our latest plan was to sneak into Moe's barn while he was gone and do a little snooping around. Sam wanted to come, too. He even assigned us all code names. Rachel was Blue 32, Sam was Green 17 and I was Red 65. Ida chose Yellow *a lot*.

Ida refused to have a number with her color. Yellow is her favorite color and "Yellow a million" didn't sound right so she insisted on Yellow *a lot*.

"We sound just like the tiny little bottles in a

box of food coloring," complained Rachel.

But Sam told us it was necessary in case we got separated and needed to call out to someone. After all, we couldn't use our real names.

Rachel, Sam and Ida were already up in the loft watching for Moe to drive away. I was held up with extra chores. Grandpa had asked me to prepare three of the empty stalls for the new horses he was getting the next day.

Interviewing people and snooping around in Moe's barn were parts one and two of our investigation. Part three was the sleepover we were planning on the night the new horses arrived at the barn.

Everyone agreed we could sleep in the barn as long as Grandpa was there to supervise. I think Grandpa mostly agreed to it because he was also curious and wanted to get to the bottom of things.

Grandpa planned to set up a cot in the office nearby. We were all hoping we'd be able to catch the horse thief in the act.

I closed the door to Nutmeg's stall and told her I'd see her in the morning. I passed Cooper Cream's empty stall next door. I thought about him often. I especially missed hearing him call out to me each day when I entered the barn to do my chores.

Tomorrow I would be competing in my first horse jumping competition with Nutmeg. When I had begun learning jumps, Cookie said that I needed to train with Nutmeg because she performed better in competitions.

But unlike Goldie, Nutmeg could sense my nervousness and seemed to take advantage of it. It was as though she was leading me and not the other way around.

I climbed up the ladder that led to Lemon Loft. Rachel, Ida and Sam were waiting for me.

"Look at the new button Charlie gave us," cried Ida as she attached it to the blue ribbon hanging on the wall. "It says...HICCUP! It says....HICCUP!"

"It says 'I'd rather be riding,'" said Sam, finishing her sentence. "And next time, don't drink so much lemonade!"

Hanging beside the ribbon was a red flier. I recognized it from the day I'd first met Rachel. It was the flier about the jamboree.

"What's that for?" I asked.

"Here," said Rachel. "I have one for you, too." She shoved the paper in my hands. "You guys never come to these and you should. They're a lot of fun. And if you don't come this time, I'm going to be really mad!"

I knew she didn't mean it. I folded the paper and tucked it in my back pocket.

"I'll ask if we can go," I told her.

"Look!" cried Sam. "He's leaving!"

We crawled over to the open window and watched as Moe's truck drove off.

"OK," said Rachel. "Operation stolen horses, part two, is about to commence*."

We scurried down the ladder and raced down the hill to Moe's barn.

Chapter Nine

CROSS YOUR FINGERS

Our voices echoed as we entered Moe's big, empty barn. It was bare and swept clean. There wasn't even a speck of hay to speak of.

"Hmmm. If Moe was the one stealing the horses, he'd probably have some hay lying around. But he doesn't," I said.

A big, old tractor was parked at the opposite end of the barn, right next to a doorway.

Sam climbed up to the loft to look around. He discovered a pulley* attached to a long cord that ran across the barn. He grabbed the pulley and held on as he flew through the air and landed abruptly on the loft at the opposite end of the barn.

"That was a blast!" he cried.

Rachel agreed that it *indeed* looked like a blast so she scrambled up the ladder to have a turn.

I was all about solving the mystery—not playing. "Come on," I told Ida. "Let's go see what's behind that door."

We passed an open doorway in the middle of the barn. Just outside was the spot where Moe usually parked his truck.

Our escape plan, in the event Moe returned, was to run out the rear door of the barn and meet at the top of the hill.

"We'd better be quick in there," I said. "If Moe returns we won't be able to cross this open door without being seen."

The door by the tractor led to an office. Inside was a desk and a large glass-front bookcase with trophies and photos of people posing beside horses.

There was one photo on the wall. I recognized a very young-looking Grandpa standing beside a man I presumed* was Moe. They were holding a trophy and smiling.

On the desk was a horseshoe paperweight and more pictures.

"There's nothing in here that would tell us

anything about the missing horses," I said. "We'd better go."

We started toward the door when all of a sudden I heard a faint rumbling, like the sound of a truck engine. It got louder and louder then came to an abrupt stop just outside the barn.

I peeked out the office door. Moe had returned sooner than expected.

Rachel and Sam had scurried down from the loft and disappeared out the back door. "Red 65, Yellow *a lot*!" Sam shouted as they ran up the hill.

"Quick!" I told Ida. "We have to hide."

I ducked behind the desk. Ida crouched* down behind the bookcase.

A few seconds later, we heard footsteps. They moved closer and closer, then came to a halt just outside the office door.

From under the desk I could see Moe's black boots that appeared gray from so much soil and dust. He paused for a second and then began to move away. I felt relieved.

But suddenly, Ida let out a giant "HICCUP!"

I crossed my fingers, hoping he didn't hear Ida…
but he did. His footsteps returned to the doorway.

I held my breath.

"Who's there?" he called out.

Ida and I remained completely frozen in our
hiding spots. I was trembling with fear.

Moe walked around to the side of the desk. I
knew he'd eventually find me so I timidly rose up
from behind it. My entire body was shaking.

"Who are you, and what are you doing in my
barn?" he asked sternly.

"I…I…..I'm Lily Anna. This is my sister Ida."

Ida stepped out from behind the bookcase. She
tried to say hello. Instead, she hiccupped.

He paused and stared at us for a few seconds.
"Where do you live?"

"Up the hill at Shelby Stables. Ted is our
grandpa." I stood there wondering if he was going
to call the police or perhaps, chase us out of the
barn with a pitchfork.

A smile formed on his face. "You're Ted's
granddaughters?" he asked, backing up to the chair

in the corner of the office. He sat down. "You look just like your mother when she was your age," he said to me. "Do you ride?"

I was still trembling. "Yes, I..."

"Your mom was a good rider."

"Red 65! Yellow *a lot*!" Rachel and Sam called out to us.

"Those your friends I saw running up the hill shouting football signals or food coloring names?" he asked.

"Yeah," Ida finally had the nerve to speak. "I'm Yellow *a lot* because I like that color *a lot*!"

He smiled. His body shook a little like he was laughing inside. "So why are you snooping around my barn?"

"We...We..." I was trying to figure out how to tell him about our investigation.

"We're trying to figure out why some of Grandpa's new horses get stolen and end up here and why you both don't speak anymore and why you have this big barn and no animals in it!" Ida blurted out.

He shook and laughed inside even more. "Well, to answer your first question, I don't know why those horses end up here. As for the second question as to why we don't speak—that's a long story. And as to why I don't have any animals here—I decided it was too much for me to take care of a barn full of horses all by myself."

Moe pointed to the photograph on the wall. "Your grandpa and I were always very close. We did everything together. But when we became adults, our opinion on things—important things—just wasn't the same."

"Red 65! Yellow a lot!"

"Those friends of yours are probably getting worried. You might want to let them know you're OK." He stood and started toward the doorway.

I didn't feel like leaving, though. I got the sense that Moe had lots of interesting stories to tell us. He seemed like a nice man. He also seemed lonely.

I paused at the doorway, remembering the red flier in my back pocket. I pulled it out and handed it to him. "We're going to this concert tomorrow night. You should come."

"I haven't been to one of these in years," he said examining the paper. Perhaps," he smiled. "Perhaps I just might."

Ida and I exited the back door of the barn. The sun felt warm and welcoming on my face.

We sprinted up the hill to find Sam and Rachel.

Chapter Ten

CHOMPING AT THE BIT

It was the morning of my first horse jumping competition. I was a bucket of nerves as we pulled into the large parking lot at the show grounds. The lucky breakfast I'd eaten earlier was sitting in my stomach, making me feel queasy*.

My new tall boots felt stiff as I stepped out of the truck. I went to the trailer to retrieve Nutmeg while Rachel and Ida ran over to check out the riding arena.

The air smelled of flowers and freshly cut grass. Girls in blue riding coats and hard hats led their horses toward the ring.

Nutmeg jerked at the reins while Mom, Cookie and I tacked her up. She stood patiently, waiting for us to finish, but I sensed she was waiting for just the right moment to start up with her misbehaving.

"There are eight jumps and one of them is a double," Rachel informed me upon her return.

Rachel had competed in jumping competitions before but more recently, her focus had been on Western-style* riding.

I placed my number on the back of my riding jacket and put on my helmet and gloves.

Everyone wished me luck as I trotted over to the ring with Nutmeg. She had a very bouncy trot.

Nutmeg chomped at the bit* as we waited for our class to be called. Soon after, a man's voice came over the loudspeaker. Ten of us trotted into the ring. I rubbed my horseshoe necklace and took a deep breath.

My legs had that wobbly feeling again as the announcer asked us all to walk, trot and canter* around the ring. That's when Nutmeg decided to misbehave. She began bucking* and refused to canter.

We hadn't even gone around the ring once when the announcer's voice called over the loudspeaker "rider 15..." That was me! "Please exit the ring!"

I was disqualified* before I even got to jump. It was a horrible moment and I was mad at myself and at Nutmeg. Cookie said it was because I still hadn't learned to control her.

I cried the entire way home.

As we pulled onto the road that led to the ranch, I vowed that the next time I competed I was going

to win.

"Cheer up," said Rachel. "You have an exciting night ahead of you."

She was right. We did have a fun night ahead of us—first, the concert and then the sleepover in the barn.

I crossed my fingers that Moe would be at the dance and that he and Grandpa would strike up a conversation.

Ida and I dressed in our prettiest dresses. Mine was pink with a white bow that tied at the waist and hers was yellow with little pinkish-white flowers that reminded me of the blossoms on the apple trees.

The entire family had decided to go, even Sam.

Cranberry Hill was a place where all the local townspeople went each month to socialize* and dance. Inside was a square, wood dance floor surrounded by round tables with white tablecloths. Strings of lights hung on the walls and long, rectangular tables were filled with every kind of food imaginable.

In front of the dance floor was a large stage—The Sugarberry Stage. On it, a band was playing, but I didn't pay much notice to it because I was busy searching for Moe. I quickly located him in the far corner of the room.

As I pushed my way through the crowd of mingling* people someone called out "Red 65, please come up to the stage."

I wasn't paying attention because I was still trying to get to Moe.

"Red 65..." a loud sigh breathed into a microphone. "Lily Anna!" someone finally shouted.

I turned toward the stage. To my surprise, Rachel was standing on it, smiling and holding a microphone. She waved excitedly.

The band continued to play while Rachel made an announcement. "I'd like you to all meet my new best friend. Come on up here Lily Anna!" she commanded.

Everyone clapped as I walked toward the

stage. I was hesitant to get up there but Rachel was persistent. "Come up and sing with me!" she insisted.

"So this is why you wanted us to come here," I whispered.

"Yep. I wanted you to be surprised. Now come on—sing with me," she said.

The band members smiled and looked on as I stood awkwardly beside her. Rachel was a good singer and very confident up on stage.

"Come on," she whispered to me. "I've heard you sing before." But I suddenly panicked. I just didn't have the courage to sing in front of a large crowd.

"I can't right now," I told her. "There's something I have to do." I climbed off the stage and disappeared into the crowd of people.

I quickly located Grandpa and took his hand. "Come on Grandpa, I want you to talk to someone," I said, as I led him over to the corner where Moe was standing.

At first the exchange between them was pleasant.

Grandpa and Moe seemed happy to see one another. Then Moe asked Grandpa about his business—big mistake!

"It's going well," said Grandpa. "We got some new horses today. I'm just hoping I don't find them in your paddock tomorrow morning."

"I'm just hoping you don't put them there and then accuse me of it," Moe replied angrily.

They argued and argued until Moe finally stormed off. What a disaster!

After the jamboree I changed quickly into my PJ's and grabbed my sleeping bag and pillow. Rachel was already in the loft, checking the batteries in the flashlights.

Sam and Ida were setting up booby traps in and around the barn. Sam hung bells on the new horses' stalls and on the barn door. Ida placed a big plastic frog in the middle of the driveway leading to the barn. When something moved in front of the frog it made a giant RIBBIT sound.

I entered the barn and checked on the new horses. They were quietly settled in for the night. Operation stolen horses, part three, was about to commence!

The sleepover was a lot of fun. We stayed up late telling scary stories, eating popcorn and, of course, singing. Ida and Rachel made up songs about all the horses in the barn.

It seemed like I had just fallen off to sleep when I was awakened by a loud RIBBIT. Rachel and Sam heard it too. Not Ida, though. She could sleep through anything.

Sam crawled over to the window and peered out.

"Do you see anything?" I whispered.

"Yeah, I...I think it's a *ghost*."

I peeked outside. A white, flowing figure was moving slowly toward the barn.

All of a sudden the bells on the door of the barn jingled.

I gasped.

We tiptoed over to the railing of the loft that

overlooked the stalls below. It was dark and we could hardly see. The white, flowing figure moved toward the stalls where the new horses were located.

Jingle, jingle. The stall door was opened. Sam crept quietly down the ladder and switched on a light.

"Grandma!" I gasped upon seeing her. She was placing a halter on the horse.

Sam stood in front of Grandma but she gazed past him as if he was invisible. Then, she led the horse toward the door.

"Grandma?" he whispered.

She ignored him and continued walking.

"I think she's sleepwalking!" said Sam.

Rachel and I scurried down the ladder. We all followed Grandma outside the barn and down the dirt road toward Moe's.

When we got to the bottom of the hill, Grandma brought the horse inside Moe's paddock and slid off the halter. Then she exited the paddock and began walking slowly back up the hill.

We decided not to startle Grandma by waking her

so we followed her back to the ranch. She walked up the stairs to her bedroom and climbed back into bed.

We were all a little stunned* as we headed back to the barn.

"She's a sleepwalker just like you," Sam joked.

"Yeah and I guess Ida's a sound sleeper just like Grandpa," I said pointing to Grandpa, snoring loudly on his cot.

⚜ ⚜

The next morning we gathered everyone together and explained what had happened.

Grandma wasn't completely sure why she was moving the horses but she had an idea.

"I guess I've always been a believer in Moe's ways of training horses," she explained. "When new horses arrive at the ranch, I secretly wish that Moe was here to work with them. He was so good with the horses."

Afterward, Grandpa went down to Moe's to retrieve his horse and explain what had happened.

Then he invited Moe back up to the ranch for coffee. We all sat on the front porch and had a good laugh.

Grandpa apologized to Moe for accusing him of stealing his horses. Then he asked Moe if he'd teach him some of his horse training skills.

Moe agreed and Grandma was very pleased.

Chapter Eleven

HOLD YOUR HORSES

"Happy Birthday to you, *Lily Anna*.
Happy Birthday to you, *Lily Anna*...."

It was my birthday and Ida decided to sing me her own version of the birthday song the entire bus ride home from school.

She was still singing as we walked up the hill past Moe's.

"Lily Anna, Ida, come here. I have something I want to show you," Moe called out to us excitedly from his barn.

Ida and I followed him inside the barn.

"Have a look," he said, motioning to the large stall near the back.

Ida and I walked toward the back of the barn. Suddenly, a horse poked its head out of a stall as if to greet us.

"Wow!" I said. "What's its name?"

"I named her Snow," said Moe as he smiled and patted her long neck.

Snow's name fit her well. She was an all-white horse with beautiful blue eyes.

"I figured one horse wouldn't be too much for me to handle."

Ida and I agreed. We were happy for Moe and we knew that Snow would be well taken care of.

Later, I entered the barn to tend to the horses, with Ida's silly birthday song still stuck in my head. I couldn't help but hum the tune to it. My mom was planning a birthday party for me after I finished my chores and did my homework.

I filled a large bucket of water while I sang the silly song. A horse at the back of the barn let out a big neigh.

"Hold on," I hollered, "I'm coming."

"Whinny, neigh!"

"Hold your horses!" I said, as I lugged the bucket down the corridor toward the impatient horse. I still wasn't sure where the noise was coming from.

The horse continued to whinny and paw at the stall door.

The closer I got the more I realized that the noise was coming from Cooper Cream's old stall.

Could it be? I wondered. *No—probably just another new horse.* I walked over and looked inside.

"Cooper Cream!" I cried upon seeing him. I was speechless! I opened the stall door and wrapped my arms around his neck. Tears began to roll down my cheeks.

"I missed you so much!" I said as I hugged and patted him.

He stood there contentedly. I knew he was glad to see me, too.

Moe appeared at the stall. "Happy Birthday, Lily Anna....A funny thing happened while I was out looking at horses. I came across a horse with the peculiar* name of Cooper Cream. I just had to to get him for you."

I stood there crying and hugging Cooper Cream.

"Thank you! If it wasn't for you, your grandpa and I would still be feuding."

Then, Cooper Cream's ears twitched upon hearing Ida, singing the birthday song.

I stepped out of the stall. Rachel was holding a cake that was glowing from all the candles on top of it. Ida, Mom, Dad, Sam, Grandma, Grandpa, Charlie and even Bagel paraded down the corridor toward us. What a birthday surprise!

cﬅ ﬊

We all sat on a blanket under the lone apple tree eating cake and ice cream while Cooper Cream happily grazed in the paddock nearby.

"I think you and that horse can qualify for the Junior Grand Prix* States next year," said Moe.

My heart skipped a beat. The Junior Grand Prix

State Championship was considered to be the most prestigious* competition in the region. All the girls who competed wore special riding jackets and were considered to be excellent riders.

"First prize is a huge trophy and a year's supply of horse feed," Rachel stated.

"I don't know if I'm ready for that," I said, still in disbelief. I never even considered that I'd be close to qualifying.

"You'll need to at least come in third in your next competition but I think you can do it," Moe said confidently. "We have a whole year to get you ready."

"And when you do qualify, you'll need something fancy to wear," added Grandpa as he handed me a brightly colored package.

I read the attached card: *Here's a good luck outfit for my good luck charm! Love, Grandpa.*

Then I tore open the package. Inside was a beautiful pink and brown plaid riding jacket with matching boots, helmet and breeches.

It truly was the best birthday ever!

Chapter Twelve

CHANGE & GROWTH

I glanced into the backseat of the truck. Rachel and Ida were singing out the back window to Cooper Cream who was following in the trailer behind us. We were on our way to my second horse jumping competition and I was determined to win this time.

Thanks to Moe, Cooper Cream was no longer spooked by dogs or the rain. He was still a little skittish* about riding in trailers, though. So Rachel and Ida tried to sooth his nerves by singing to him.

I'd given him a nice bath that morning and braided his soft mane. And when it came time to lead him into the trailer, he followed me in. He snorted a few times, though, to let me know he wasn't happy.

I'd completely settled in to my new life at Shelby Stables. I felt like a different person from a year ago when we first arrived—more confident and a little less superstitious. I even surprised Mom when I requested pancakes that morning instead of my usual "lucky breakfast." I knew I didn't need it to do well.

And at the competition, Cooper Cream and I did, *indeed*, do well. We cleared every jump and took home the blue ribbon. I couldn't wait to hang it on the wall of our fort along with my new winning number—17. *Grand Prix States here we come!*

Afterward, I gave Cooper Cream his favorite

treat—half an apple—for being such a good partner.

We all decided we should go to the concert that night to celebrate. But on the drive home we realized there was one small problem. Rachel had developed laryngitis* from singing all day to Cooper Cream.

Ida, who's used to singing all the time, happily volunteered to take her place.

I stood near the stage and watched as Ida held the microphone and prepared to sing. The band started to play. Ida opened her mouth and then…froze. She stood on stage, wide-eyed, unable to move or speak.

Rachel whispered to her from the side of the stage, "Come on Ida. We need you!"

But Ida wouldn't budge.

I knew I had to do something. So I took a deep breath and walked up on the stage. I removed the microphone from Ida's hand and began singing along with the band.

Rachel was surprised, but grateful. And Ida just stood there beside me, stiff as a board. *Wow*, I thought, *I really am a different person than I was a year ago.*

❧ ☙

Later that evening, I went to the barn to say goodnight to Cooper Cream. I told him all about the jamboree and how I'd gotten up the courage to sing in front of everyone. He pricked his ears and listened intently.

The moon was shining down on the lone apple tree outside the barn. The seeds my mom helped me plant beside it had grown into a tiny seedling*. *How amazing,* I thought, *that something so small and unimportant could turn into something so wonderful.*

I patted Cooper Cream and thanked him for doing such a great job earlier that day. "We did it!" I told him. "Now we can compete in the Grand Prix States." He blinked.

Then, Grandpa poked his head inside the barn. "Your mom's looking for you," he said. "She told me to tell the next Grand Prix Champion jumper it's her bedtime."

I pictured myself wearing my lucky pink and brown plaid riding jacket and holding up the winning trophy. "We'll nail every jump and win again," I whispered to Cooper Cream. Then I kissed him goodnight.

Cooper Cream and I—champion jumpers. I liked the sound of that.

As I walked out of the barn, I paused and knocked on wood...*just in case*!

Glossary

*Many words have more than one meaning. Here are the definitions of words marked with this symbol * (an asterisk) as they are used in sentences.*

bay: *a horse with a reddish-brown coat color and black mane and tail*

bit: *a metal mouthpiece that is part of the bridle*; used to control a horse while riding*

blaze: *a wide, white stripe running down a horse's face*

board: *(boarding) keep a horse in a stable which provides space, care and feeding for a fee*

bridle: *a harness that fits over a horse's head; used to help control or guide the horse while riding*

briskly: *quickly, full of energy*

broken (in): *tamed and trained to be ridden*

brownstone: *a house with a stairway leading*

to a front entrance on the second level

bucking: *leaping and raising the hind legs in the air*

canter: *a three-beat gait* of a horse, faster than a trot*, slower than a gallop**

chomping: *(chomped) chewing, biting into something*

commence: *to start or begin*

commotion: *noise or disturbance*

crouched: *stooped low to the ground with knees bent*

dappled: *a white/gray horse with darker, spotted markings*

disqualified: *removed from a contest*

drastically: *considerably, a lot, extremely*

feud: *an argument or quarrel that's been going on for a long time*

forged: *moved ahead, moved along*

gait: *step, way of walking*

gallop: *the fastest gait* of a horse*

girth: *a strap used to hold a saddle* in place*

Grand Prix: *the highest level of show jumping,*

in which riders compete for an important prize

graze: *to feed on growing grass*

groggy: *dazed from just waking up*

halter: *a harness that fits around the horse's head and allows the horse to be led or tied*

hoisted: *raised or lifted up*

intimidated: *frightened or scared*

jamboree: *a large gathering for a concert or festival*

laryngitis: *dry, sore throat; loss of voice*

lead line: *a long, thin leather strap that attaches to a horse's halter*, used to control and lead the horse*

loft: *a room or storage area (above the barn) with a sloped roof*

lunge line: *a long leather strap used to exercise a horse*

lunge: *using a lunge line* to exercise a horse around you in a circle*

mingling: *(mingle) joining or mixing with others in a crowd*

muttered: *spoke in a low voice or grumbled*

neigh: *a horse cry or whinny**

obsessed: *focused on one thing or idea*

paddocks: *fenced in areas for horses*

passed away: *died*

pasture: *a large area covered with grass*

peculiar: *odd, different*

pellets: *small, solid balls*

perky: *happy and cheerful*

plot: *a piece or area of land*

potluck: *a party where each guest or family brings food to share*

prestigious: *important or popular*

presumed: *thought or guessed something to be true without knowing for sure*

pulley: *a wheel attached to a line that carries weight from one point to the another*

queasy: *uncomfortable, sick feeling in stomach*

ranch hand: *a person who's hired to perform duties on a farm*

reared up: *stood on hind legs with front hoofs in the air*

reins: *straps that fasten to the bit* on a bridle* to help control and direct a horse*

rugged: *rough looking, with strong features*

rummaged: *searched or looked through contents*

saddle: *a leather seat that fastens to a horse's back for riding*

saddle pad: *a blanket placed under the saddle* to protect the horse's back*

scally cap: *a flat rounded cap made of wool, tweed or leather, with a small brim*

scenario: *image or example*

seedling: *a young plant grown from a seed, not yet three-feet high*

skittish: *nervous, uneasy*

socialize: *to speak or mingle* with others*

spacious: *large, roomy*

stirrup: *a ring attached to the saddle to support the rider's foot*

stunned: *surprised, amazed*

superstitious: *having beliefs that go against what is generally thought of as true*

symbolized: *stood for something such as an idea or meaning*

tack: *riding gear such as saddle*, saddle pad* and bridle**

tack up: *to fit a horse with riding gear*

traditional: *a longtime customary or usual thing to do*

trot: *a two-beat gait* of a horse, faster than a walk, slower than a canter**

Western-style (riding): *differs from traditional* English-style in equipment, riding style and clothing. At the most basic level, Western-style requires the rider to hold the reins with one hand instead of two. The clothing worn in Western competitions is more decorative and sparkly, and the saddles are larger and designed for long days of riding.*

whinny: *a horse cry or neigh**

Horse Speak
Understanding and Listening to a Horse

Horses are remarkable animals. They are capable of showing emotion, understanding, fear and even trust. The most important thing a human can do when dealing with horses is to be kind and respectful toward them. Here are a few tips to help you understand and communicate with your horse:

Know the signs

Signs a horse is anxious or upset:

- Ears pinned back
- Head high with moving feet
- Eyes opened wide, may see eye whites
- High-pitched whinnying or neighing

Signs a horse is relaxed or happy:

- Blinking
- Head hanging low
- Chewing
- Licking lips
- A horse resting one hoof slightly on hoof tip

Signs a horse is listening to you:

- Blinking
- Ears twitching or pricked forward

Know the sounds

Horse sounds and what they mean:

- Nicker with a slight raise of head: usually happy
- Snorting: afraid or excited
- Neighing: high-pitched means horse is upset, lower pitched, shorter sounds means horse is trying to tell you something
- Sighing: horse is relaxed

Know what they like

(Be sure to check with an adult before attempting these):

- Having necks scratched and massaged
- Treats such as carrots, peppermints, apples, sugar cubes, hay cubes
- Singing
- Speaking to them in a kind tone and manner

Know how to approach a horse

Horses have a blind spot in front of their nose. Approaching a horse head-on may frighten it. Walk slowly toward a horse from the side.

Know how to lead

Working with your horse:

- Horses are smart and can sense if you're nervous or lacking in confidence. Relax and display self-assurance when working with a horse.
- It's important that you let the horse know that you're in charge. Being in charge means leading a horse in a respectful manner.

Important: Do not attempt any of the above instructions without adult supervision and permission from the horse owner.

About the Author

Julie Driscoll keeps a notebook with her at all times because everywhere she goes, something funny or exciting happens that she knows would make for an interesting story.

Her greatest inspirations are her two daughters, Emily and Kerry and her husband, Steve, who's a lot like a little kid trapped inside a grown-up's body.

Mrs. Driscoll is a writer and artist. She has written a screenplay in the family genre and a television pilot for a local network.

*In addition to **Adventures at Shelby Stables**, Mrs. Driscoll has written **The Note in the Piano** and **Blizzard on Moose Mountain**.*

A special thanks from the author to the following people:

Betty and Kay from Woodsong Farms
Nicole, Alexis and Brenna MacDonald
Olivia Scannell and all the girls from Creed Crossing Farm
Gina, Maggie, Nichole and Caitlin from Briggs Stables
Jen, Olivia and Gayle Corcoran
Alexia Madeloff
Delphine Bosworth
Holly Kosel
Emily and Kerry Driscoll
Chelcee Agraz